THIRD-GRADE DETECTIVES #4

The Cobweb Confession

THIRD-GRADE DETECTIVES #4

The Cobweb Confession

George E. Stanley
illustrated by
Salvatore Murdocca

ALADDIN PAPERBACKS

NEW YORK LONDON TORONTO SYDNEY SINGAPORE

This book is dedicated to the wonderful students in Mrs. Schlueter's third-grade class at Lincoln Elementary School in Norman, Oklahoma. You're great! Thanks for all your help.

First Aladdin Paperbacks edition July 2001

Aladdin Paperbacks
An imprint of Simon & Schuster
Children's Publishing Division
1230 Avenue of the Americas
New York, NY 10020

Designed by Steve Scott

The text for this book was set in 14-point Lino Letter.

Manufactured in the United States of America

20 19 18 17 16 15 14 13 12

Library of Congress Catalog Card Number: 2001-022942

ISBN-13: 978-0-689-82197-4
ISBN-10: 0-689-82197-2

Chapter One

Todd Sloan looked around Mr. Merlin's classroom.

Where is Noelle? he wondered.

He yawned big.

He was still sleepy.

Jonathan, his father's friend from college, was visiting his family.

Jonathan was sleeping in Todd's bed.

Todd was sleeping on the living-room couch.

It wasn't very comfortable.

Just then, Noelle rushed inside.

She handed Mr. Merlin a tardy slip.

Todd wondered why she was so late.

They usually walked to school together.

Noelle took her seat next to Todd.

"What happened to you?" Todd whispered. "Why didn't you walk to school with me?"

Noelle opened her mouth.

She showed Todd a big hole where a tooth used to be.

"I tripped over Rover this morning. I had to go to the dentist," Noelle said. She raised her hand. "Mr. Merlin! I have something really exciting to tell everyone!"

"What is it, Noelle?" Mr. Merlin said.

"There's a thief in town. He broke into our house," Noelle said. "I talked to the police about it this morning."

Mr. Merlin raised an eyebrow. "Really?"

Noelle nodded.

"He got in through the basement steps at the back of our house.

"He stole my mother's silverware."

Noelle looked over at Todd.

"He even stole some things from your house. But he didn't get in through your basement," she said. "Your mother thinks he climbed in through a window in your room."

"What?" Todd cried. "Why didn't Mom tell me about it this morning?"

"You had already gone to school when she discovered it," Noelle said.

"What did he steal?" Todd asked.

"Your baseball cards," Noelle said.

Todd couldn't believe it.

He had just looked at his baseball cards last night.

He had them out because Jonathan wanted to see them.

"Could we help the police find the thief?" Misty Goforth asked Mr. Merlin. "Could we help them solve the mystery?"

Mr. Merlin thought for a minute.

"Perhaps Mr. Merlin's Third-Grade

Detectives could help in some way," he said.

"But I'll have to think about how you can do it.

"Now we need to work on science.

"We're going to study spiders."

"Yuck!" several kids said.

"No! No! Spiders are very interesting," Mr. Merlin said. "I've studied them for years.

"But we're only going to study the kinds of spiders that live in cobwebs."

Amber Lee Johnson raised her hand.

"I thought all spiders lived in cobwebs," she said.

"No, Amber Lee," Mr. Merlin said.

"Some spiders live in holes in trees.

"Some spiders live in holes in the ground.

"But most spiders live in cobwebs, and those are the ones we're going to study.

"So for homework, I want you all to look for cobwebs after school.

"Try to find as many as you can.

"Tomorrow, we'll talk about where you found them.

"Then I'll tell you how to mount the best one so you can bring it to class.

"But it has to be a cobweb that no spider is living in now.

"I don't want you to tear down a cobweb that a spider is still using."

Todd shuddered.

He didn't like spiders.

He didn't want to have anything to do with them.

Besides, he had more important things on his mind.

He wanted to catch the thief who'd stolen his baseball cards.

"Not all cobwebs are alike, either," Mr. Merlin continued.

"Different kinds of spiders make different kinds of cobwebs.

"That's what we're going to study.

"I want you to learn to recognize each type of cobweb.

"That way you'll know what kind of spider lives there."

Noelle raised her hand.

"Yes, Noelle?" Mr. Merlin said.

"Don't spiders trap bugs in their cobwebs and then eat them?" Noelle asked.

"Yes, they do," Mr. Merlin replied.

"Well, if I were a spider, I'd trap that thief who broke into my house and turn *him* into food!" Noelle said.

The class laughed.

Todd knew he'd never want to be a spider.

But he wished he could think of some way the class could help the police catch the thief.

He wanted to get his baseball cards back.

Chapter Two

"Why did that thief steal my baseball cards?" Todd asked his mother.

"Thieves usually steal things they can sell, Todd," his mother said. "Your baseball cards are worth a lot of money."

Todd sighed and changed the subject.

"I want my room back, Mom. How much longer is Jonathan going to stay with us?"

His mother shrugged. "I know it's hard sleeping on the couch, but your father wants Jonathan to be comfortable. They haven't seen each other in years."

"Why did he decide to visit us now?" Todd asked.

"Jonathan was driving from New York to Oregon," his mother said. "We were on the way."

"I don't think Dad likes him very much," Todd said.

"That doesn't matter," his mother said. "I want you to be nice to Jonathan. He's our guest."

"Okay," Todd said.

But he didn't feel like being nice to Jonathan.

In fact, he didn't feel like being nice to anybody.

His mother wouldn't even let him go into his room while Jonathan was staying with them.

She said Jonathan liked his privacy.

So, Todd decided he'd go across the street to Noelle's house.

Nobody had taken *her* room away from her.

He found Noelle in the kitchen.

She was eating cookies and drinking a glass of cold milk.

"I'm just glad that thief didn't steal anything that belonged to me," Noelle said.

Todd started to tell her that she didn't have anything worth stealing.

But he didn't.

She knew he was in a bad mood.

He didn't want to start an argument with Noelle.

He didn't want her to tell him to go home.

He wouldn't have any place to go when he got there.

"Do you want to look for cobwebs?" Noelle asked.

"You know I hate spiders, Noelle," Todd said. "I wish Mr. Merlin wasn't making us do this."

"I think it's a neat idea," Noelle said. "I like spiders."

"Well, I don't want to look for cobwebs

now," Todd said. "I want to think of a way to catch the thief."

He stood up to leave.

"If you change your mind, I'll be down in our basement," Noelle said. "It has cobwebs all over it."

"Okay," Todd said.

When Todd got outside, he saw a police car parked in front of Mrs. Ruston's house.

Mrs. Ruston was one of the fourth-grade teachers at his school.

She was standing on her front porch.

She was talking to Dr. Smiley and Mr. Merlin.

Dr. Smiley was a police officer.

She used science to solve crimes.

She was also a friend of Mr. Merlin's.

Todd and Noelle were sure they were a couple.

Mr. Merlin's class had helped Dr. Smiley solve a lot of mysteries before.

Todd decided to find out what was going on.

"Hi, Mrs. Ruston! Hi, Dr. Smiley! Hi, Mr. Merlin," he said. "What happened?"

"A thief broke into my house. He came in through the basement," Mrs. Ruston said. "He stole some of my valuable rings."

"He broke into our house, too," Todd said. "He stole my baseball cards."

"But we'll catch him, Todd," Dr. Smiley said.

"Mr. Merlin's Third-Grade Detectives will help you, too, won't they, Todd?" Mr. Merlin said.

Todd nodded. "I'd rather catch the thief than look for cobwebs. I hate spiders."

Mrs. Ruston and Dr. Smiley looked puzzled.

Mr. Merlin explained the class project.

He looked at Todd.

"I'll give you a secret-code clue in the morning," he said. "It'll tell you how you might be able to catch the thief."

Chapter Three

Todd was waiting for Noelle so they could walk to school together.

He was beginning to get mad because she was late again.

Suddenly, Noelle ran out of her house.

"Guess what?" she cried. "That stupid thief also stole my ring!"

"Really?" Todd said.

Noelle nodded. "My grandmother gave that ring to me. I wanted to wear it today. I just discovered it was missing."

"Now you know how I feel," Todd said.

They started walking to school.

Noelle hardly said a word.

Todd could tell that she was really mad.

"That dumb thief also messed up my cobwebs!" Noelle finally said. "Now I'll have to take a broken one to class."

Oh, no! Todd thought. He had forgotten to look for a cobweb.

"What do you mean?" he asked.

"The thief came in through our basement window. It used to have cobwebs all over it," Noelle explained. "Now the good ones are all gone. The thief probably has them all over him. He only left broken ones."

Todd hoped Mr. Merlin didn't ask him if he had looked for cobwebs.

He knew there weren't any in his basement.

His parents cleaned their house from top to bottom every Saturday.

When Todd and Noelle finally got to school, Misty and Johnny were talking to Mr. Merlin.

The thief had also stolen Johnny's watch and Misty's bracelet.

He got in through Johnny's basement window.

He got in through Misty's back basement steps.

When everyone was seated, Mr. Merlin wrote the secret-code clue on the chalkboard:

MPPL GPS DPCXFCT

"This will help you catch the thief," Mr. Merlin said.

Everyone copied it down quickly.

Todd hoped he could solve it right away.

He wanted to catch the thief and get his baseball cards back.

Mr. Merlin gave them fifteen minutes to work on the secret-code clue.

But that wasn't enough time for Todd or anyone else.

Sometimes Todd wished Mr. Merlin

wouldn't change the secret codes each time he gave them a secret-code clue.

But he always did.

Mr. Merlin said solving secret codes made the class think better.

"Well, put your secret-code clues away for now," Mr. Merlin said.

"I'll give you a rule for it later.

"Now we need to talk about our science project."

Noelle raised her hand.

"I looked for cobwebs in our basement," she said. "But that thief messed all the good ones up."

Several other kids said the same thing happened to them.

"I'm sorry," Mr. Merlin said. "But you can find cobwebs in other places besides basements."

Amber Lee raised her hand.

"Yes, Amber Lee?" Mr. Merlin said.

"The thief didn't break into our house.

So there are still a lot of cobwebs in our basement," Amber Lee said. "I didn't see any spiders living in them, either."

"That's good," Mr. Merlin said. "Those are the kinds I want you to bring to class."

"I tried to get some last night," Amber Lee said. "But they all fell apart."

"I'm going to tell you how to keep that from happening," Mr. Merlin said.

"First you get a piece of cardboard.

"It should be a little bigger than the cobweb.

"Next you glue a piece of dark cloth to one side of it.

"Then you put the cardboard with the cloth behind the cobweb and pull the cardboard toward you.

"That way the cobweb will stick to the cloth.

"And it will already be mounted when you bring it to school."

"That sounds easy," Misty Goforth said.

Yeah, Todd thought. *Maybe it wouldn't be*

so bad after all. At least, he'd never have to touch the cobweb.

But how would he know if a spider still lived in it? he wondered.

He'd probably pick a cobweb where the spider had just left home for a few minutes.

Suddenly, Todd saw himself being attacked by a spider that came back home and saw what Todd had done to his house.

Todd didn't want to fight a spider for a silly school project.

"I want you to bring in all kinds of different cobwebs," Mr. Merlin continued.

"There are dome-shaped webs.

"There are flat webs.

"There are triangular webs.

"And there are orb webs.

"Orb webs are round.

"That's what the common garden spider makes.

"Those are the cobwebs most people see.

"The design of the cobweb depends on the type of spider.

"And some spiders only live in certain states.

"We can only study the cobwebs of the spiders that live in our state."

Mr. Merlin talked to them some more about spiders and their cobwebs.

Then they did math and reading.

When they finished, Mr. Merlin gave them a rule for the secret-code clue:

"If you move over one seat to the right, the person in the last row will be in the first row."

Todd thought for a minute.

All right! he thought.

Now he was sure he knew what kind of secret code Mr. Merlin was using for this clue.

Chapter Four

The recess bell rang.

Todd and Noelle rushed out of the classroom.

Misty and Johnny were right behind them.

They ran toward the big oak tree at the edge of the playground.

"I wish I knew how to solve the secret-code clue," Johnny said. "I want to catch that thief!"

"Me, too!" Misty said. "I'm so mad that he stole my new bracelet."

"My dad gave me that watch for my birthday," Johnny said. "Now it's gone."

"It's okay. I know how to solve the secret-code clue," Todd said when they got to the tree. "Mr. Merlin's rule was easy this time."

"What does it say, Todd?" Noelle asked.

"I'll show you," Todd said.

He picked up a stick.

"These codes are called shift codes," he explained.

He wrote out the regular alphabet in the dirt.

"Now, I'm going to write another alphabet underneath this one," he continued.

"But I'm going to *shift* it one place to the right."

"Why?" Johnny asked.

"Mr. Merlin's rule says that if one student moves over one seat to the right," Todd explained, "the student in the last row will be in the first row.

"He's talking about the alphabet.

"*A* is the first student.

"*Z* is the last student.

"You move *A* in the second alphabet over one *seat*.

"Then you write it under the *B* in the first alphabet.

"That pushes all of the letters over one place.

"Now the *Z* in the second alphabet is under the *A* in the first alphabet.

"So *Z* is now in the *first row*."

Todd finished writing out the second alphabet in the dirt.

"Now we can solve the secret-code clue," Noelle said. "Now we can catch that thief!"

Todd looked at the piece of paper on which he had written the secret-code clue:

MPPL GPS DPCXFCT

Then, working together, the four of them solved it.

"Look for cobwebs!" Noelle cried. She thought for a minute.

"That has to be a mistake."

"I think you did something wrong," Misty said. "What do cobwebs have to do with catching the thief?"

"Yeah," Johnny said. "That's our science project."

Todd knew they were all disappointed in him.

But he didn't know what else to do.

He was sure the secret code was a *shift* code.

But the clue didn't make any sense.

The bell to end recess rang.

The four of them headed slowly toward Mr. Merlin's classroom.

When everyone was seated, Noelle said, "We solved the secret-code clue, Mr. Merlin. But you must have made a mistake."

"Oh, really?" Mr. Merlin said. "What do you think the clue says?"

"It says 'Look for cobwebs,'" Todd said.

"But that's right," Mr. Merlin said. "I think

you can catch the thief if you look for cobwebs."

Todd couldn't believe it.

He couldn't stand spiders.

He couldn't stand cobwebs.

But if he wanted to find the thief who stole his baseball cards, he'd have to look for them anyway.

Chapter Five

The next morning, Mr. Merlin was disappointed.

Only Amber Lee and Noelle brought cobwebs to class.

"We couldn't find any," several other kids said.

Mr. Merlin sighed.

Amber Lee waved her hand excitedly.

"Yes, Amber Lee?" Mr. Merlin said.

"We can look for cobwebs in my basement," Amber Lee said.

"They're everywhere!

"My parents never clean down there.

"It's really spooky, too."

Mr. Merlin thought for a minute.

"Well, you'll need to ask your parents first, Amber Lee," he said. "They might not want us to do that."

Amber Lee gave Mr. Merlin a big smile. "I already have," she said.

"My mother said I could have a cobweb party after school today.

"Everyone in the class is invited.

"And when we all have our cobwebs, we can go back upstairs and eat spider cookies.

"My mother's baking them now!"

Todd shivered.

He liked to go to parties.

But he didn't want to go to this one.

He could just see himself all covered in cobwebs!

"Why, that's a wonderful idea, Amber Lee!" Mr. Merlin said.

"I'll make sure everyone has permission to go.

"I'll also bring enough cardboard and dark cloth for everyone to use.

"Now, we'll do our spelling and math."

But Todd couldn't think about anything except getting cobwebs all over him.

Finally, the last bell rang.

Everybody was supposed to be at Amber Lee's house at 4:30.

Todd and Noelle started walking home.

"I feel sick," Todd said.

"No, you don't," Noelle said. "You just don't want to go to Amber Lee's cobweb party."

"Whoever heard of having a cobweb party?" Todd said. "That is so dumb."

"I think it'll be fun," Noelle said. "Now I won't have to use my broken cobweb.

"And I can hardly wait to eat one of those spider cookies.

"Anyway, Todd, Mr. Merlin said looking for cobwebs will help us catch the thief."

Todd sighed.

Noelle was right.

He'd just have to forget how much he hated spiders and cobwebs.

He'd have to remember how mad he was at the thief for stealing his baseball cards.

Chapter Six

Amber Lee met Todd and Noelle at her front door.

Mr. Merlin and the rest of the class were already down in the basement.

Todd thought Amber Lee had described the place perfectly.

There really were cobwebs everywhere.

In fact, it looked like a haunted house.

"I'm glad you finally made it," Mr. Merlin said. "There are some really interesting cobwebs down here."

"I can tell," Todd said weakly.

"We have to be careful, though," Mr.

Merlin added. "There are spiders still living in a lot of them."

Todd gulped.

He was suddenly mad at Amber Lee for telling Mr. Merlin that no spiders lived in these cobwebs.

"It's hard to see down here, Mr. Merlin," Todd said. "Can we turn on more lights?"

"There's only one light," Amber Lee said. "It's already on."

Todd looked at the bare lightbulb hanging in the center of the basement.

It lit a small circle of the room right underneath it.

It left most of the room in darkness.

Unfortunately, that was where most of the cobwebs were.

Mr. Merlin gave each person a piece of cardboard with dark cloth glued to it.

"I brought some flashlights," he said. "We'll take turns using them."

Suddenly, Todd had an idea.

His parents were always telling him he needed to be more polite.

Well, now was his chance.

He'd let *everybody* in the class go ahead of him to use the flashlights.

Maybe there wouldn't be any good cobwebs left when it came his turn to look.

"I think Todd should go first," Amber Lee said. "He solved the secret-code clue."

"No! That's not polite!" Todd cried. "I want to be polite!"

Mr. Merlin gave him a puzzled look.

"My parents like me to be polite," Todd said in a calmer voice. "I think other people should go first."

Mr. Merlin smiled. "Well, that's very nice of you, Todd," he said. He turned to the rest of the class. "Who wants to go first?"

Noelle and Amber Lee raised their hands.

They were joined by Johnny, Leon, and Misty.

"You'll need to choose partners to hold your flashlights," he said. "You can't hold the flashlight and mount your cobwebs at the same time."

Amber Lee chose Johnny.

Misty chose Leon.

"I want Todd for my partner," Noelle said.

Oh, great! Todd thought. How was he going to get out of this now?

Then he thought of something.

If he was holding the flashlight, he couldn't mount his cobweb.

He'd ask Noelle to do it for him.

"Okay," he said.

Just then, Mr. Merlin said, "But you can't ask your partner to mount your cobweb for you. You have to do it yourself."

Mr. Merlin handed the flashlights to Todd and the rest of the partners.

"Come on, Todd," Noelle said. She pointed to the darkest corner in the basement. "I think there are lots of good cobwebs over there."

Noelle started toward the far corner.

Todd was right behind her with the flashlight.

But when they got out from under the ceiling light, they could hardly see anything.

"I think this battery is weak," Todd said. "We won't be able to see if there are any spiders on the cobwebs."

"Hurry up, Todd! And quit complaining!" Noelle whispered. "I want to make sure that we get some good cobwebs."

There was junk stacked everywhere.

Todd and Noelle had to squeeze between a lot of old furniture and dusty cardboard boxes to get to the corner.

But they finally made it.

"It *is* kind of dark over here, isn't it?" Noelle said.

"I told you so," Todd said. "Do you want to wait for a better flashlight?"

"No," Noelle said. "We don't have time."

Todd shone the flashlight all around.

He had never seen anything like it before.

This whole side of the basement looked like a huge cobweb.

Suddenly, he was short of breath.

What if he got trapped inside this monster cobweb?

What if there were hundreds of spiders just waiting to turn him into food?

Something touched the back of his neck.

He screamed.

He dropped the flashlight.

Now they couldn't see anything.

"What happened?" Noelle said.

"There are spiders all over me!" Todd cried.

He started flailing his arms in the air.

He could feel the giant cobweb wrapping around him.

It was on his hands.

It was in his hair.

It was in his eyes.

It was covering his nose and his mouth.

Now he couldn't breathe.

"Stay calm, Todd! Stay calm! We'll get the cobweb off of you!"

Todd recognized Mr. Merlin's voice.

Mr. Merlin pulled the cobweb away from Todd's nose.

Now Todd could breathe again.

Mr. Merlin pulled the cobweb away from Todd's eyes.

Slowly he opened them.

"Are you okay?" Mr. Merlin asked.

No, I'm not! Todd thought.

He couldn't believe how embarrassed he felt.

What a disaster this had been!

He was sure he'd never hear the end of it.

Everybody in school would know that

he was afraid of little old spiders.

"I guess so," he finally managed to say.

All of a sudden, a door opened at the rear of the basement.

Everyone turned to look.

A shadowy figure appeared.

"Who can that be?" Amber Lee whispered. "Nobody ever uses those back steps. The door is always locked."

Chapter Seven

"Jonathan!" Todd exclaimed.

Jonathan seemed startled when he saw everyone looking up at him.

"Who is that?" Noelle whispered to Todd.

"He's my father's college friend," Todd whispered back. "He's the one who's sleeping in my room."

Jonathan came on down the steps.

He brushed cobwebs away from his face and his clothes.

"I rang the front door bell, but no one answered," Jonathan said.

"My mother's probably watching a game

show on television," Amber Lee said. "Those things are so loud."

Jonathan looked around.

"Are you guys having a party down here?" he asked. "It's a bit early for Halloween, isn't it?"

"It's a school project," Todd explained. "We're collecting cobwebs."

"Well, that sounds interesting," Jonathan said.

But Todd could tell by the tone of Jonathan's voice that he didn't really think it was.

"What do you want, Jonathan?" Todd asked.

"I'm going to treat you and your parents to dinner tonight," Jonathan said. "I came by to ask you where you'd like to eat."

"Oh, that's easy! *Mr. Goober's!*" Todd said. "It's a pizza place where they have all kinds of video games."

"Then Mr. Goober's it is," Jonathan said. "I'll tell your parents that's where we're going."

"Lucky!" several of the kids said to Todd.

Jonathan started up the back basement steps.

"You can go out the front way," Amber Lee said. "We never use those back steps."

"That's okay," Jonathan said. "I don't want to disturb your mother's game show."

Todd watched Jonathan disappear into the darkness at the top of the steps.

"I wish we had company visiting us," Noelle said. "I'd give up my room to go to Mr. Goober's."

"Me, too," Amber Lee said.

"Well, let's get back to our project," Mr. Merlin said.

But when they started looking for cobwebs again, there weren't many good ones left.

"It's all Todd's fault," Amber Lee complained. "There would have been plenty for all of us if he hadn't messed them up."

"Yeah, Todd," Leon said. "I've got a really lousy cobweb because of you."

"Me, too," Misty said.

"I didn't do it on purpose," Todd said.

"Don't worry, class. There are other cobwebs in town," Mr. Merlin said. "I'm sure the rest of you will be able to find at least one somewhere around your house."

"The spider cookies are ready!" Amber Lee's mother called down to them.

Mr. Merlin and the class hurried upstairs.

They all washed their hands.

Amber Lee's mother gave them each two spider cookies to eat.

But Todd couldn't even eat one.

He thought it tasted like the cobwebs he had gotten in his mouth.

Finally, it was time for everyone to go home.

"Bring your cobwebs to school tomorrow," Mr. Merlin said. "We'll start studying them."

"Will you let me get a cobweb from your basement?" Todd asked Noelle. "I don't care if it is broken."

"We don't even have broken ones now," Noelle said.

"What happened to them?" Todd asked.

"Mom told Dad to clean up the basement," Noelle said. "She was embarrassed when the police were down there looking for clues. She didn't even want me to keep the broken one I mounted."

"Well, where am I going to find one now?" Todd said. "I need it before school tomorrow."

Noelle shrugged.

"You have to help me, Noelle," Todd said.

"Well, I could probably help you find one if I had some of Mr. Goober's pizza," Noelle said.

Todd stopped. "That's a great idea!" he said. "I'll ask if you can come with us tonight."

When Todd got home, he found his parents sitting in the living room.

"May Noelle go with us to Mr. Goober's?" he asked.

"Oh, honey, we're not going to Mr. Goober's after all," his mother said.

"Why not?" Todd asked.

"Jonathan forgot something important he had to do," his mother replied. "He said he might be gone for several hours."

Todd was really disappointed.

His mouth was all set for some of Mr. Goober's pizza.

"Mom? How did Jonathan know I was at Amber Lee's house?" he asked.

His mother shrugged. "He must have overheard you talking about the party," she said.

That's funny, Todd thought. He didn't

remember seeing Jonathan around.

Todd left the living room.

He went straight to his room.

He didn't care what Jonathan thought about it, either.

Todd wanted some privacy, too.

One of Jonathan's suitcases was on top of his bed.

The suitcase was old and dusty.

Yuck! Todd thought.

He reached for the handle to lift the suitcase off his bed.

The suitcase fell open.

The contents spilled out.

There were sweaters and shirts and slacks. There were socks and ties. There were also a couple of watches and a ring.

Uh-oh! Todd thought.

He started to put everything back inside.

But just then a spider crawled out from between two sweaters.

"Yikes!" Todd cried.

The spider raced across his bedspread and disappeared.

Todd shuddered.

What was a spider doing inside Jonathan's suitcase? he wondered.

Then Todd saw the most wonderful thing in the world.

A cobweb!

The spider had spun it on one of Jonathan's sweaters!

Chapter Eight

Todd got a coat hanger from his closet.

He carefully lifted up Jonathan's clothes.

He didn't see any more spiders.

Todd couldn't believe his luck.

Somehow a spider had gotten into Jonathan's suitcase in New York.

It had spun a web on one of his sweaters.

It had probably been in Jonathan's basement for a long time.

It's a wonder it didn't have more spiders in it, Todd thought.

He shuddered.

A New York spider was hiding somewhere in his room.

Todd was almost glad he was sleeping on the couch.

Maybe by the time Jonathan left, the spider would be gone, too.

Todd held the sweater up to the light.

Now he had a mounted cobweb.

He was sure Mr. Merlin wouldn't mind if he brought the whole sweater to class.

After all, it was cloth, too.

And if he tried to take the cobweb off, Todd was sure that he'd ruin it.

He wasn't about to do that.

Suddenly, Todd wondered if Jonathan would let him take the sweater to school.

Well, why wouldn't he? Todd decided.

After all, Jonathan was sleeping in his room.

It was only fair.

Besides, Jonathan wasn't here for him to ask now.

But if Todd told his mother, she'd probably

get mad at him for looking in Jonathan's suitcase.

Todd would have to hide the sweater until tomorrow, so he could take it to school.

But where? he wondered.

He thought about it for a couple of minutes.

Of course! he finally decided.

He'd ask Noelle to keep it.

He didn't think she'd mind.

He had to tell her they weren't going to Mr. Goober's anyway.

He took the sweater and slipped out the back door.

He ran across the street to Noelle's house.

"I found a cobweb!" Todd told her.

He showed Noelle the front of Jonathan's sweater.

"It's perfect!" Noelle said. "It's better than all those dirty old cobwebs in Amber Lee's basement."

"But I need to hang the sweater in your closet tonight," Todd said. "I don't want Mom to know I have it."

"Why?" Noelle asked.

"I don't want her to know I opened Jonathan's suitcase," Todd said.

"Okay," Noelle answered.

They went to Noelle's room.

Noelle hung Jonathan's sweater in her closet.

"We're not going to Mr. Goober's tonight, either," Todd said. "I'm sorry."

"That's okay. I couldn't go anyway," Noelle said. "I have to go get a new pair of shoes."

The next morning, Noelle met Todd at her front door with the sweater.

They walked to school together.

When they got to their classroom, Todd showed Mr. Merlin the cobweb on the front of Jonathan's sweater.

Mr. Merlin studied it carefully.

"This is really interesting, Todd," he said. "Where did you get it?"

Todd told him about Jonathan's suitcase.

"It's a New York spider. It doesn't live in our state," Todd said. "Is that okay?"

"Of course, Todd. It's a perfect cobweb," Mr. Merlin said. "I think you'll find out some really interesting things about it, too."

"Class! Let's get started!" Mr. Merlin said. "We have a lot to do today!

"First, I want you to draw a picture of your cobweb."

He held up a big book.

"When you've finished, we'll look in here to see what type of spider made it.

"It lists all of the spiders found in every state and shows pictures of their cobwebs."

When the class finished their drawings, they all looked in Mr. Merlin's spider book.

Everyone found an exact picture of his or her cobweb.

Everyone except Todd.

"Why isn't my cobweb in your book?" he asked Mr. Merlin. "I looked in the chapter about New York spiders."

Mr. Merlin didn't answer him.

Instead, he started writing on the chalkboard.

Chapter Nine

"I'm going to give you a secret-code clue to tell you why," Mr. Merlin said.

That's strange, Todd thought.

Mr. Merlin only gave them secret-code clues to help them solve police crimes.

Why was he giving them one now?

Mr. Merlin wrote:

RKLLQ IKHVEM CQ YPKH S QKTRBEPJ
QRSRE

"You may work on this for a few minutes, then we'll do spelling," he said.

The class started working on the secret-code clue.

Todd used all of the secret codes that Mr. Merlin had ever given them.

But he still couldn't solve it.

Neither could anyone else.

Finally, Mr. Merlin said, "It's time to do spelling."

He wrote the day's spelling words on the board.

The class copied them onto their papers.

They took turns spelling them to each other.

They took turns writing them on the board.

But when Mr. Merlin wasn't looking, Todd tried to solve the secret-code clue.

He had been so excited when he had found the cobweb.

Now he was disappointed.

He wanted to know why his wasn't in Mr. Merlin's big spider book like everyone else's.

By the end of the day, Todd still hadn't solved the secret-code clue.

When he got to his house, Jonathan was in the living room talking to his parents.

They all looked at him.

"Todd, someone opened Jonathan's suitcase. Now one of his sweaters is missing," his mother said. "Do you know anything about it?"

Uh, oh! Todd thought. He swallowed hard.

"I took it to school," he said.

Jonathan gave him a funny look.

"Why did you do that?" his father asked.

"I needed a cobweb for my class project," Todd said. "The sweater had a perfect one on the front of it."

"It did?" Jonathan said.

Todd nodded.

"I think you owe everyone an explanation, son," his father said.

Todd took a deep breath.

"It all started because I missed being in my room," Todd began.

"Jonathan was gone, so I went in there to read some comics.

"His dusty old suitcase was on my bed.

"I started to move it, but it fell open.

"Everything spilled out.

"A spider ran out from between some of the clothes.

"It had spun a cobweb on one of the sweaters."

Todd looked at his mother.

"The spider is still loose in thc house," he added.

Todd's mother gasped.

"This is all my fault," Jonathan said.

"I stored my suitcase in the basement of my apartment building in New York City.

"I should have checked it more carefully for spiders before I packed."

Todd was glad he hadn't.

"Yes, you may use the sweater for your school project," Jonathan said.

"Thank you," Todd said.

"You probably also saw my surprises," Jonathan said.

Todd nodded.

He remembered the watches and the ring.

"What surprises?" his father asked.

"I brought you all some presents," Jonathan said. "I just haven't had time to wrap them yet."

He went to Todd's room.

When he came back, he had the watches and the ring.

He gave Todd and his father each a watch.

He gave Todd's mother the ring.

"Oh, this is so nice of you, Jonathan," Todd's mother said.

"It sure is, Jonathan," Todd's father said.

Todd looked at his watch.

It had something engraved on the bottom.

It said, *Birmingham, Alabama*.

That must be where it was made, Todd thought.

"Thanks, Jonathan," he said.

"You must be the only one in your class with a New York cobweb," Jonathan said.

Todd shrugged. "I don't think the spider is really from New York," he said. "I looked in the New York chapter of Mr. Merlin's big spider book, but I couldn't find it."

Jonathan turned pale. "Really?" he said. "That's strange."

Todd thought it was strange, too.

He didn't know what he was going to do.

Everyone had to identify his or her cobweb in order to get a grade.

The next day at school, Mr. Merlin asked, "Has anyone solved the secret-code clue yet?"

No one had.

"That's too bad. It will tell you why Todd couldn't find his cobweb in the New York chapter of my spider book," Mr. Merlin said. "It may also help you catch the thief."

Todd and Noelle looked at each other.

"Give us a rule, Mr. Merlin!" Noelle said.

"Okay," Mr. Merlin said.

On the chalkboard, he wrote:

USE MY FRIEND'S LAST NAME AND THEN FINISH WITH WHAT'S LEFT.

Chapter Ten

"You may work on the secret-code clue with each other," Mr. Merlin said. "But try not to be too loud."

Todd and Noelle moved their desks together.

Todd quickly got out a sheet of paper.

"Mr. Merlin's friend is Dr. Smiley. We have to start with her," Noelle said. She thought about that for a minute. "What does that mean?"

"Here's what I think it means," Todd said.

On his sheet of paper, he wrote: SMILEY.

"I think this is a secret code that uses a KEY WORD.

"That means you write out the KEY WORD first.

"If you have duplicate letters, then you leave all of them out of the word except for the first one.

"SMILEY doesn't have duplicate letters.

"There's just one of each.

"Then you finish out the alphabet with the letters that are left."

Next to SMILEY, Todd wrote: ABCDFGHJ-KNOPQRTUVWXZ.

"So the secret code alphabet is SMI-LEYABCDFGHJKNOPQRTUVWXZ?" Noelle asked.

"Yes," Todd said.

"Now what?" Noelle said.

"You write the regular alphabet underneath the secret code alphabet," Todd said.

He quickly did that.

"The regular alphabet is called the *clear* alphabet."

Todd looked at the secret code message again: RKLLQ IKMVEM CQ YPKH S QKTRBEPJ QRSRE.

"In order to decode this, you look below each letter in the secret-code alphabet.

"That will give you the letter it stands for in the clear alphabet."

"*R* stands for *T, K* stands for *O, L* stands for *D,* so that's two *D*'s, and *A* stands for *S*. *Todds*."

Noelle looked.

"You don't use apostrophes in secret codes, so that's *Todd's,*" Todd said.

Then they quickly translated the rest of the secret-code message:

TODD'S COBWEB IS FROM A SOUTHERN STATE.

"How can your cobweb be from a southern state if Jonathan brought the spider from New York?" Noelle said.

Todd thought for a moment.

"Maybe he didn't," Todd said.

He suddenly remembered what was written on the back of his watch.

He raised his hand.

"Yes, Todd?" Mr. Merlin said.

"May I borrow your big spider book?" Todd said. "I want to look at the chapter on Alabama."

Mr. Merlin smiled. "Of course." He handed it to Todd.

Todd quickly got out the drawing he had made of his cobweb.

He turned to the chapter on Alabama spiders.

Finally, he saw a picture of his cobweb.

"There it is!" Todd cried. "The spider that made my cobweb lives in Alabama and three other southern states."

"What do you think that proves, Todd?" Mr. Merlin said.

Todd took a deep breath.

"I think it proves that the spider in Jonathan's suitcase didn't come from New York," Todd

said. "Jonathan wasn't telling the truth."

Suddenly, Todd remembered Jonathan's coming down the back steps of Amber Lee's basement.

"Jonathan's the thief!" he cried.

"He didn't come over to Amber Lee's house to see me.

"He came over to steal things.

"That's how he got into all the houses!

"He came in through the basement!

"Except in our house.

"Because he was already there!"

"That's why I told the class to look for cobwebs," Mr. Merlin said. "I thought the thief might have them on his clothes."

"He did!" Noelle said.

Mr. Merlin smiled. "You're right, Noelle. But I wasn't talking about clothes in a suitcase. I was talking about clothes he was wearing after each robbery. Todd's the one who really solved this mystery."

"What's going to happen to Jonathan?" Todd asked.

"The police are talking to him now," Mr. Merlin said.

"What do you mean?" Todd asked.

"I recognized your cobweb, Todd," Mr. Merlin explained.

"I knew it was made by a spider found in only four southern states.

"I told Dr. Smiley about it.

"We both wondered why Jonathan told you the spider came from New York.

"Dr. Smiley talked to the state police in the four southern states.

"The police in Alabama told her about a thief who had broken into homes all over their state.

"Dr. Smiley told them she thought it might be Jonathan.

"The local police are at your house right now, Todd.

"They're going to take Jonathan in for questioning."

Todd wished he weren't in school now.

He wanted to be at his house to watch the police take Jonathan away to jail.

Two days later, Dr. Smiley stopped by Mr. Merlin's classroom.

A policeman from Alabama was with her.

"I want to thank Mr. Merlin's Third-Grade Detectives for helping us solve this mystery," the policeman said.

"We've been looking for Jonathan for a long time.

"All of the stolen property he took from houses here has been recovered.

"But he had already sold what he stole in Alabama." He looked at Todd. "Except for two watches and a ring."

"If Todd hadn't found the cobweb on the front of Jonathan's sweater," Dr. Smiley added, "Jonathan probably never would have been caught."

The class applauded.

Todd felt himself blushing.

He was glad he had helped the police.

But he hoped this was the last spider mystery that Mr. Merlin's Third-Grade Detectives ever had to solve.

Catch a "thief" with fingerprints!

Cobwebs are the "fingerprints" of spiders. Different spiders make different kinds of webs, so they have different fingerprints. People have different fingerprints, too. No two are alike. Ask your teacher to help you prove this with the following activity:

1. You will need to fingerprint everyone in your class. Here's how to do it:

- **a.** Draw as many two-inch squares on pieces of white paper as there are students in your classroom. Make sure you have one extra square.
- **b.** Write each of your classmate's names at the bottom of a square. Leave one square blank.
- **c.** Turn a pencil sideways and rub the graphite on a piece of white paper.
- **d.** Have each classmate put his or her right forefinger in the graphite and roll it gently from side to side.

e. Have each classmate hold up his or her forefinger so you can put a piece of clear tape on the graphite.

f. Remove the tape gently and stick it in the square above the person's name.

2. When you have finished fingerprinting the class, leave the room.

3. While you're gone, your teacher will name someone to be a thief and fingerprint the "thief" as described in #1 above, putting the taped fingerprint on the blank square.

4. You will come back into the room and solve the mystery.

HOW? Well, each person's fingerprint is made up of lines called loops, whorls, and arches. By comparing the "thief's" fingerprint with the rest of your classmates' fingerprints, you should be able to give the thief a name!